WALKING WITH DINOSAURS
THE 3D MOVIE
3D
HANDBOOK

By Calliope Glass

HARPER FESTIVAL
An Imprint of HarperCollinsPublishers

HarperFestival is an imprint of HarperCollins Publishers.

Walking with Dinosaurs Handbook
BBC, BBC Earth and Walking with Dinosaurs are trademarks of the British Broadcasting
Corporation and are used under license.
Walking with Dinosaurs logo © BBC 2012
BBC logo © BBC 1996

Library of Congress catalog card number: 2013934067
ISBN 978-0-06-223288-5
Typography by Gene Vosough
13 14 15 16 17   LP/RRDC   10 9 8 7 6 5 4 3 2 1

First Edition

A LONG, LONG TIME AGO . . .

The Earth is very old, much older than the dinosaurs. The story of Earth's history began 4.54 billion years ago, when our planet was molded out of the gas and dust left over from the formation of the sun.

About 1 billion years after Earth formed, conditions were finally ripe for the first living creatures to develop. The oldest animals were simple—sponges and jellyfish with soft bodies made up of only a few different kinds of cells—but larger and more complex species evolved by 600 million years ago. The first vertebrates were fish that lived in the oceans, alongside invertebrates such as trilobites and other shelled animals. About 370 million years ago, vertebrates first ventured onto land.

About 250 million years ago, the Age of Dinosaurs began.

Back then, all sorts of creatures roamed the Earth's surface and filled the skies. Many of them were dinosaurs, but not all of them. There were turtles, lizards, mammals . . . and even birds!

Hello there! Pleased to meet you. The name's Alex—Alex the Alexornis. I'm going to be your guide on this incredible journey through time. I have an amazing story to tell you about some friends of mine who lived hundreds of millions of years ago. But they weren't birds like me. . . .

They were dinosaurs.

ALEXORNIS BIRDS

Birds evolved from dinosaurs long before the dinosaurs went extinct. The oldest known bird fossil is still the iconic Archaeopteryx from Late Jurassic Germany. This fossil is about 150 million years old. During the Mesozoic, one unusual group of birds dominated the skies. These were the enantiornithines, the so-called "opposite birds." They were given this name because many features of their skeleton are different from living birds. For example, many species still had teeth and claws on the wings, which living birds lack. Enantiornithines were very common during the time of dinosaurs. More than fifty species have been found. One of these is *Alexornis*.

CHAPTER 1

Our story begins on a beautiful spring day on the Arctic plain.

The wind whistled through my feathers as I soared down out of the clouds toward the lush forest below. I was on my way to the place where the Pachyrhinosaurus made their nests and raised their young. Most of the eggs in the Pachyrhinosaurus nests had already hatched, but the babies were still young. The adults roamed through the nesting ground, keeping watch for predators. Their big feet made a slow thunder on the ground as they walked—the adults were enormous.

Pachyrhinosaurus lived in large herds, so there were many of these huge dinosaurs at the nesting ground—and many, many eggs and babies in the nests.

DINOSAUR EGGS

All dinosaur species laid eggs. Dinosaur eggs are common fossils, and sometimes they are even found with the small bones of embryos inside. Different dinosaurs produced different types of eggs. But no matter what shape, no known dinosaur egg is larger than about the size of a football. This means that all dinosaurs, even the mightiest species like *Tyrannosaurus* and *Brachiosaurus*, were tiny when they hatched. Dinosaur eggshells are often found as broken pieces. Sometimes entire eggs are discovered, and rarest of all is a complete nest. Some fossilized dinosaur nests have been found. There are even a few fossil nests that have been found with a parent on top. The good mother (or father, because in many living bird species fathers care for the eggs) must have died protecting the still unhatched young. Some dinosaur species had vast nesting grounds that parents would return to year after year to lay eggs and begin raising their families. We know this because, in a few exceptional cases, huge numbers of nests are found together, spread out over hundreds of square miles. One of the most famous of these is a site in Argentina called Auca Mahuevo, which contains thousands of sauropod eggs. Eggs are so common that it is impossible to walk there without stepping on eggshells. You can hear the crunch of eggs under your feet as you walk between the fossilized nests!

I liked the Pachyrhinosaurus, and they liked me. That's because they hated the bugs that buzzed around their heads, and I loved those bugs!

I loved eating them, that is.

The Pachyrhinosaurus were happy to let me fly around them, picking those pesky insects right off of their huge frills—that's what the big bony ruffs around their heads were called. We Alexornis had an understanding with these dinosaurs. They got pest control, and we got lunch!

There were plenty of baby Pachyrhinosaurus in the nesting grounds that spring. It was hard to imagine that these tiny babies would grow up to be as huge as their parents. After they hatched from their eggs, the young stayed in the nest for a while with their siblings. Pachyrhinosaurus mothers brought them food.

On this particular day, I watched a mother Pachyrhinosaurus feeding her babies in the usual way—by giving them predigested food to eat. That certainly wasn't what *I'd* like for lunch. But then again, I eat bugs, so I guess I'm not one to judge.

The babies were so cute! In my head I started giving them names. The one who had hatched first was the biggest. He had a fierce look on his face. This was "Scowler." He was always the first to get his dinner because he could push his brothers and sisters out of the way.

The smallest hatchling in the nest was "Patchi." To tell you the truth, he wasn't very impressive. That poor little guy was never at the front of the line for dinner. I watched him as he was butted out of the way by his brothers and sisters again and again. No wonder he was so small—he never seemed to get a full meal!

I didn't think he stood much of a chance.

Or so I thought. But every so often, someone comes along and changes the way you think. For me, that was Patchi.

Patchi wasn't having much luck getting dinner. The rest of his siblings had crowded him out. They chowed down on their meal while Patchi scrambled around the nest, trying to wedge himself into the crowd.

Then things went from bad to worse. A big, dark shadow rose up at the edge of the nest.

PACHYRHINOSAURUS

Pachyrhinosaurus was just one of many species of ceratopsids—the horned and frilled dinosaurs—that lived in North America during the latest Cretaceous, the final few million years of the Age of Dinosaurs. A close cousin of *Pachyrhinosaurus* is *Triceratops*, one of the most famous dinosaurs of all. Like *Triceratops*, *Pachyrhinosaurus* was a large plant eater that walked on four legs and had a huge skull with horns. It was something like a dinosaur version of a bull.

The first fossils of *Pachyrhinosaurus* were discovered in 1946 in Alberta, Canada, by the legendary fossil hunter Charles M. Sternberg.

Later scientists continued to find new skeletons of *Pachyrhinosaurus*. Today three distinct species are recognized, including one that lived only in the cold and dark polar regions of Alaska.

It was a Troodon! These predators snuck into the Pachyrhinosaurus nesting ground every now and then, looking for a quick snack. I fluttered back as fast as I could. Troodon were scary. They moved fast, and they were always hungry.

And they'd just as soon eat an Alexornis as a baby Pachyrhinosaurus.

TROODON

The small, fast, smart dinosaur *Troodon* is one of the closest relatives of birds. *Troodon* itself lived during the final 12 million years of the Cretaceous Period and ranged across North America, all the way up to the polar highlands of Alaska. Teeth of *Troodon* were some of the first dinosaur fossils ever found in North America. When they were found in the 1850s, these teeth were mistaken as the teeth of lizards. It took almost a hundred years for scientists to recognize that they belonged to an unusual type of birdlike dinosaur.

Troodontids were close relatives of dromaeosaurids, the familiar group of small, fierce theropods like *Velociraptor* and *Deinonychus*. The size, skeletons, and behavior of troodontids and dromaeosaurids were very similar. Members of both groups were adapted for speed, as they had light skeletons with long legs. Both groups had a large, sharp, sickle-shaped claw on each foot. And both had long-snouted skulls with large eyes and a huge brain. They were stealth fighters—the dinosaur version of Navy Seals or Black Ops.

Troodon itself has the largest brain relative to its body size of any dinosaur that has ever been studied. Its brain was about the size of a tennis ball, which is pretty large for a dog-sized dinosaur. In comparison, the huge long-necked sauropods had much smaller brains, only about the size of a walnut. Imagine that—a nut-sized brain for an animal larger than a bus! Compared to these sauropods, as well as most other dinosaurs, *Troodon* was a genius. It was a dinosaur Einstein!

The diet of *Troodon* has been the subject of much debate among scientists. The speed-adapted skeleton, large eyes and brain, and deadly foot claws all suggest that *Troodon* was a meat eater. But the story may not be so simple. The teeth of *Troodon* are very unusual for a carnivore. They are not the thin, knifelike teeth with tiny serrations that are commonly seen in *Velociraptor*, *Allosaurus*, and most dinosaur predators. Instead, *Troodon* teeth are thick and have large serrations—called denticles—lining the front and back edges. These features are more common in plant-eating dinosaurs and reptiles, and this is why the teeth of *Troodon* were originally mistaken for those of a lizard. It is likely that *Troodon* was able to eat both meat and plants. This type of animal is known as an omnivore.

The moment the babies in the nest spotted the Troodon, they scrambled away, fast. But it was too late for little Patchi. Before he could even move, the Troodon snapped him up in its jaws!

I watched in horror as the Troodon ran off with Patchi. The little Pachyrhinosaurus dangled helplessly—the Troodon had grabbed him by the frill. The Troodon looked around nervously as he ran. There was a good reason for him to be nervous. He was in the middle of a huge Pachyrhinosaurus nesting ground . . . and the adults did not take kindly to predators near their young.

Sure enough, a bellowing female Pachyrhinosaurus loomed in front of the Troodon. He was dwarfed by her huge body. She roared angrily, blocking his path. The Troodon swerved away and ran on, but everywhere he turned there was another angry adult Pachyrhinosaurus. Meanwhile, Patchi squirmed and wiggled in the Troodon's jaws, but he couldn't get free. The Troodon raced for the freedom of the forest.

And that's when Bulldust arrived. He was the leader of this particular Pachyrhinosaurus herd, and he was also Scowler and Patchi's father. He blocked the Troodon's escape route and pawed the ground, snorting angrily. Powerful muscles rippled under his leathery, scarred skin.

If I had been that Troodon, I would have been scared senseless. Bulldust was not a dinosaur to mess with.

The Troodon started to go in one direction, then tore off in another. Troodon are fast, and they know it—but Bulldust was fast, too. He blocked the Troodon again and again. The Troodon skidded, slid, and spun—and finally, he lost his grip on Patchi! Patchi went flying into the underbrush and the Troodon made his escape.

I watched as Patchi landed in a bank of ferns, tumbling head over heels. Bulldust hadn't seen where he landed, so Patchi was all alone as he shook his head and found his feet again. I heard the distant *crash* of Bulldust wandering off in the other direction, still looking for Patchi.

CHAPTER 2

Patchi looked around. His frill had been torn by the Troodon and a small beam of light shone through. He set off to find his family, but he didn't have much luck. A tiny little guy like that, well—I already told you I didn't think he stood a chance. Patchi staggered around the nesting grounds, first following one adult Pachyrhinosaurus, then another . . . none of them was his mother. But Patchi was plucky—and playful! A dragonfly whizzed by his head and the little fellow went off chasing it, all his cares forgotten.

Patchi followed that dragonfly right into the jaws of an Alphadon—snap! The Alphadon gobbled up the dragonfly and peered curiously at Patchi. She wasn't

ALPHADON

Alphadon was a type of marsupial that lived in North America during the latest Cretaceous Period, about 70–66 million years ago. It is known almost entirely from fossilized teeth, which are just a few millimeters long. Scientists can only guess at the appearance of the rest of the skeleton, but based on the size of its teeth it was likely that *Alphadon* was about as big as a rat. Its teeth are similar to those of modern-day omnivorous mammals, which eat both plants and meat. Marsupials like *Alphadon* were very common during the Late Cretaceous Period, but were devastated by the end-Cretaceous extinction that killed off the dinosaurs. *Alphadon* itself went extinct, as did most of its closest relatives. Only a few marsupials survived, which evolved into the kangaroos and possums of today's world. So *Alphadon* can be thought of as something like a great-great-grandfather (or, more accurately, a very old cousin) of the kangaroos!

used to seeing a little Pachyrhinosaurus out by himself. Patchi stared back just as curiously—he'd never seen an Alphadon! Her glossy fur was the softest-looking thing he'd ever seen. Patchi followed the Alphadon down a worn track in the underbrush until she slipped away, too fast for him to follow.

Just then, a shadow fell over Patchi. He looked up and realized the Alphadon had led him right in between the enormous, treelike legs of an Ankylosaurus. Patchi stared up at the great, scaly face of the Ankylosaurus, and it stared down at him. Slowly, it lowered its face toward Patchi, trying to get a better look at this strange visitor.

Patchi panicked and scrambled away as fast as his short little legs could take him. Panting for breath, he

ANKYLOSAURUS

Ankylosaurus looked something like a military tank. That is the simplest analogy to describe this most bizarre type of dinosaur. Its entire body was covered with thick, bony armor. The end of its tail was a giant club that could be swung from side to side. This was a dinosaur you wouldn't want to mess with. It lived alongside *Tyrannosaurus rex*, but even the fearsome tyrant dinosaur king probably avoided *Ankylosaurus* at all costs.

Ankylosaurus was a large and strong animal. Adults were probably about twenty to thirty feet long, about six and a half feet tall at the hip, and weighed five to six tons. They walked on all fours and probably moved very slowly, at most just a few miles per hour. A sturdy, armored animal like *Ankylosaurus* didn't need to run fast to escape from predators. If it was threatened, it could probably just hunker down and wait for a predator to exhaust itself trying to break through the bony armor. Some living armored animals such as armadillos behave this way.

The club at the end of the tail was about the same size as the skull. It was heavy like a bowling ball. Computer models have shown that animals like *Ankylosaurus* could swing their clubs at fast speeds, quick and powerful enough to break the bones of any predator or rival they came into contact with. *Ankylosaurus* probably used its tail club like a medieval mace—a club with a heavy ball at the end of a stick, which knights used to bludgeon their opponents during battle.

charged down a winding maze of tracks leading through ferns and brush, until he emerged out of the forest and into a beautiful valley with a lagoon in its center.

It was the most beautiful thing he had ever seen in his short life. Patchi skidded to a stop, and caught his breath while he looked around him in awe. The sunlight sparkled on the quiet water of the lagoon, and ferns rippled like waves in the gentle breeze. Everywhere, dinosaurs roamed in quiet herds. Across the lagoon,

pterosaurs pecked at the ground with their long beaks, foraging for food.

Patchi wandered farther into the valley, heedless of the danger he was in. Being out in the open is never safe for a young dinosaur, especially one so far from his nesting ground—and his mother.

Sure enough, it wasn't long before a family of hungry Hesperonychus caught sight of Patchi. These fearsome hunters began stalking the young Pachyrhinosaurus right away. Patchi noticed them, almost too late, and fled.

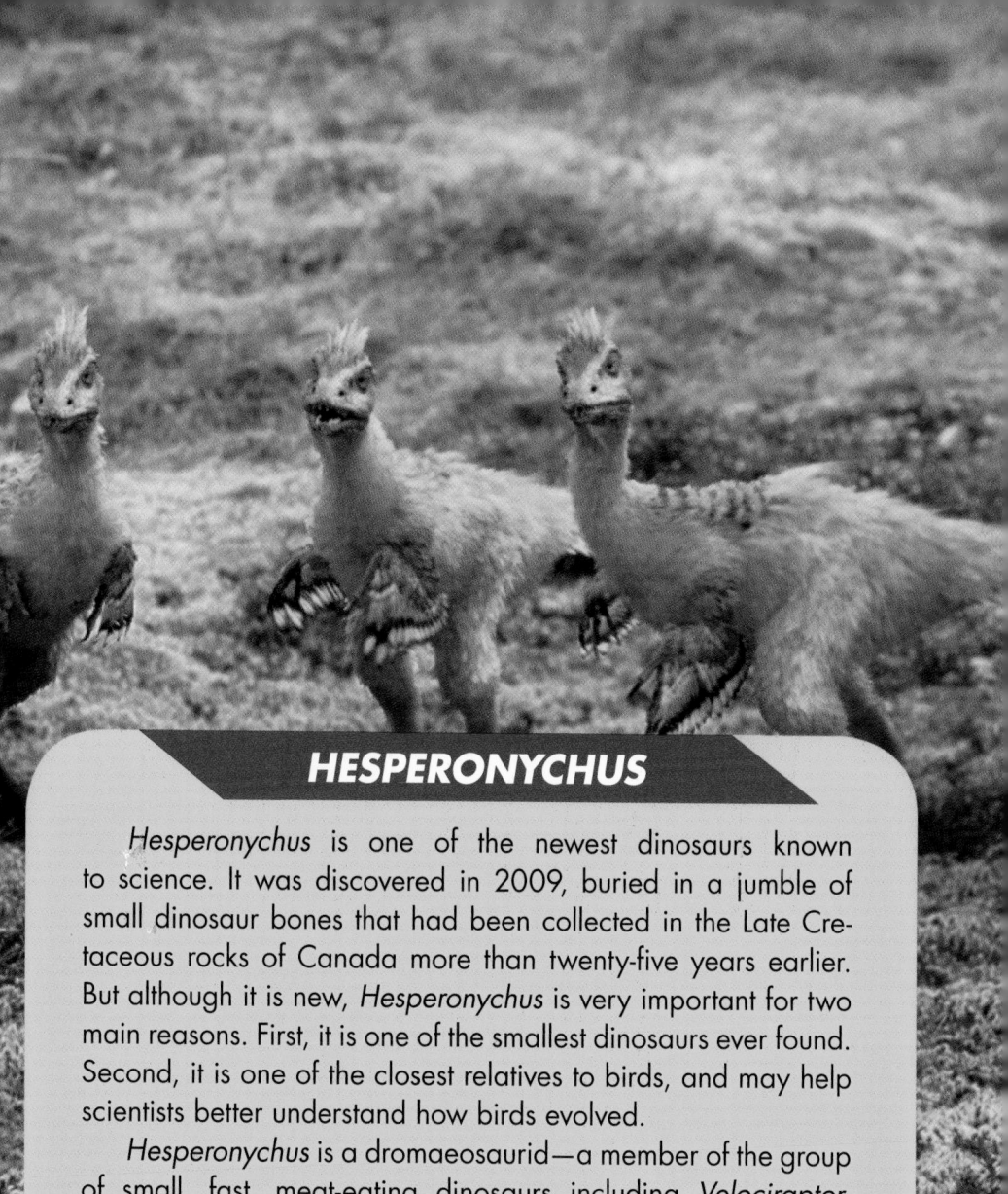

HESPERONYCHUS

Hesperonychus is one of the newest dinosaurs known to science. It was discovered in 2009, buried in a jumble of small dinosaur bones that had been collected in the Late Cretaceous rocks of Canada more than twenty-five years earlier. But although it is new, *Hesperonychus* is very important for two main reasons. First, it is one of the smallest dinosaurs ever found. Second, it is one of the closest relatives to birds, and may help scientists better understand how birds evolved.

Hesperonychus is a dromaeosaurid—a member of the group of small, fast, meat-eating dinosaurs including *Velociraptor*, *Deinonychus*, *Microraptor*, and *Rahonavis*. Most dromaeosaurids range from about the size of a human down to the size of a poodle. But *Hesperonychus* was much smaller: It was probably only one to two feet long from head to tail and weighed as little as two to four pounds. *Hesperonychus* would have looked like a killer chicken! It is clear proof that not all dinosaurs were giant monsters like *Tyrannosaurus* or *Brachiosaurus*.

Heart pounding, Patchi made for the trees again. But the Hesperonychus were fast . . . too fast! They were closing in on their little prey when, out of nowhere, Patchi was snapped up and heaved into the air. The Hesperonychus ran away, and Patchi squirmed desperately. He was sure he'd been caught by another Troodon—or maybe something even worse! But when he twisted around to catch sight of his captor, he realized that he'd been caught by his very own mother!

Patchi breathed a big sigh of relief. He'd never been so happy to see his mom!

Patchi swung happily from his mother's beak as they made their way back to the nesting ground. He was surprised by how nearby it seemed from high up. His mother's long, swaying strides ate up the distance. Soon, Patchi heard the familiar calls of his siblings. He kicked his legs, eager to rejoin them in the nest.

Patchi's mother lowered him to safety with his brothers and sisters. Patchi curled up happily in a warm, soft corner of the nest. What an adventure he'd had! His thoughts spun around and around as he remembered the smells, sounds, and astonishing sights he'd encountered during his short trip out of the nest.

From my perch above the nesting grounds, I looked down at Patchi in his nest. Had I said he didn't stand

a chance? Now I wasn't so sure. In fact, I was pretty impressed by the little Pachyrhinosaurus.

Maybe he was born under a lucky star. Or maybe there was something special about him. Either way, he had survived his first day out of the nest.

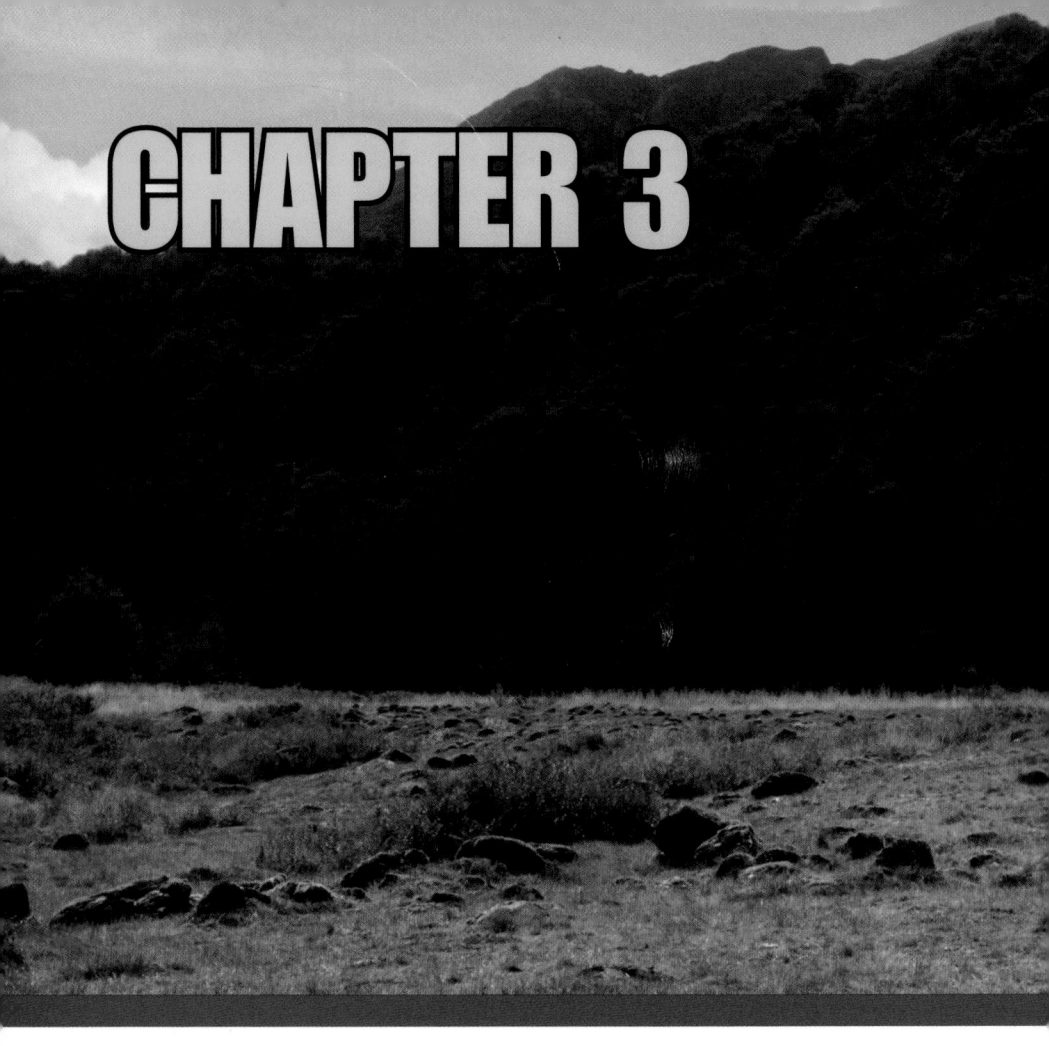

CHAPTER 3

Time passed.

Spring slid into summer. Up in the Arctic Circle, the summer sun never set. It glided around the horizon at the peak of summer, bathing the trees and ferns in light both day and night. The plants leafed out and shot up, growing fast.

HOW YOUNG DINOSAURS GROW

How did some dinosaurs like *Tyrannosaurus* and *Diplodocus* become so big? Many years ago, scientists viewed dinosaurs as cold-blooded and lazy creatures. It was thought that huge dinosaurs achieved their large size by growing very slowly but living a very long time, maybe even over a hundred years. By constantly growing throughout their lives, dinosaurs would eventually become massive. This is basically how living crocodiles grow.

But like so many older ideas about dinosaurs, this turns out not to be true. Dinosaurs actually grew very quickly from a tiny hatchling into a full-bodied adult. Small dinosaurs, such as *Troodon* and *Velociraptor*, would have reached full size in just a few years at most. Much larger species such as *Tyrannosaurus rex* would have taken longer to grow into adult size, but probably no more than about twenty years. Even the most colossal dinosaurs of all, the long-necked sauropods, probably didn't live to be much older than fifty or sixty years old, and grew to their full size long before this time. The rapid growth rates of dinosaurs are another similarity shared with living birds, which grow faster than any other vertebrates (animals with backbones). Many birds take only a few weeks to grow from a hatchling into an adult!

How do scientists know these things about dinosaurs? The secrets of dinosaur growth are locked away deep inside their bones. If you cut open a dinosaur bone, take a very thin slice, and look at it under a microscope, you can see growth rings. These are just like the rings in a tree trunk. One ring is formed every year, during the winter months when the bone stops growing because food is scarce. This means that you can tell the age of a dinosaur fossil by counting the number of growth rings!

Scientists have counted the rings of many dinosaurs. These rings are widely separated from each other deep inside the bone, meaning dinosaurs grew fast when they were young. But they are closer together toward the edges of the bone, showing that growth slowed as full size was reached. And never—not once—have scientists counted anywhere near a hundred growth lines. So dinosaurs could not live for more than a century! In fact, when it comes to *Tyrannosaurus rex*, no single fossil has ever been found with more than thirty growth rings. So *T. rex* became huge by growing really fast for a short amount of time.

The dinosaurs grew fast, too. Soon Patchi and his brother Scowler were big enough to leave the nest. They spent their days exploring the nesting ground and playing. Pachyrhinosaurus use their frills like horns, charging their enemies or rivals and knocking them over with their strong, bony heads. Patchi and Scowler practiced charging each other pretty often— and Scowler always won. Patchi might have good luck, but that didn't change the fact that he was small for a Pachyrhinosaurus. No matter how much he grew, Scowler always grew more.

As I watched the two brothers play and grow, it became clear which of them was likely to follow in Bulldust's footsteps as the leader of the herd. Scowler was bigger, stronger, and more aggressive. Patchi was sweet, smart, and curious, but he was no match for his brawny brother.

PACHYRHINOSAURUS FRILLS AND HORNS

The most distinctive feature of *Pachyrhinosaurus* is its elaborate skull, which was covered in horns and bumps of many different sizes and shapes. All ceratopsids had a long snout at the front of the skull and a huge, thin, platelike frill at the back. Most species also had some types of horns. But the details of the horns were different in each species. *Triceratops* had three large horns: one over each eye and one above the nose. This was not the case in *Pachyrhinosaurus*. Instead, the parts of the skull above the eyes and nose were covered with a mass of thick, rough bone. These are called "cranial bosses." They are basically huge bumps, and they probably would have been covered with keratin, the same material that makes up our fingernails. *Pachyrhinosaurus* also had a few horns, but these were smaller than those of *Triceratops* and located far back on the skull, on the frill.

What was the purpose of these horns and cranial bosses in *Pachyrhinosaurus* and other ceratopsids? They probably weren't primarily used to defend against predators like *Tyrannosaurus* or *Gorgosaurus*. The horns and bosses of ceratopsids usually were not present on the skulls of young individuals and appeared during the teenage years. If they were used for protection, it wouldn't make sense for the young, small, and weak juveniles to lack them. Instead, the fact that the horns and bosses show up when the animal was going through puberty and getting ready to mate is good evidence that they were used to attract the attention of mates, or to scare off potential rivals who may want to fight over a mate. They also could have been used to push around rivals during such fights, just as male bison today will often charge one another and lock horns to compete for a mate.

When Patchi wasn't play-fighting with Scowler, he loved to explore. I guess his early adventure with the Troodon had made a strong impression!

One day, in late summer, Patchi followed a butterfly to a stream where hundreds of other butterflies gathered to drink from the damp rocks. Patchi edged close to the water at the base of a small waterfall. The butterflies swarmed up, clouding the air with color as they left. It was a breathtaking sight, and Patchi was so distracted by it that it took him a moment to realize he wasn't alone.

Patchi looked down at the stream. His reflection was joined by another reflection—there was another young Pachyrhinosaurus standing above him, at the top of the waterfall. Their eyes met in the water.

Her name was Juniper, and she was the same age as Patchi, but from a different herd.

POLAR DINOSAURS

Dinosaurs lived all across the world and in many environments. Their fossils have been found on all continents, even Antarctica.

One of the most interesting discoveries of the past few decades is that many dinosaurs lived in the cold and dark polar regions, at the very top and bottom of the Earth. Climates were warmer during the Age of Dinosaurs than they are today. There were probably no glaciers during this period, but the North and South poles would still have been quite cold. And they would have been very dark during most of the winter and light during much of the summer, just like today.

Soon after Patchi met Juniper for the first time, the days began to get shorter. The summer was ending. Pterosaurs took flight for their southern Winter Ground. Clouds gathered in the sky. The wind turned cold. Fall was coming, and winter would come after that. Winter in the Arctic Circle was dark, cold, and miserable.

Bulldust knew it was time to head south. He could smell it in the air. Every year, he led his Pachyrhinosaurus herd south from the nesting grounds to their winter home in warmer territory. Now, he began gathering his herd together to begin the trip again.

The great migration had begun.

CHAPTER 4

Bulldust's herd moved slowly but steadily. Many other herds were traveling with them. This was Patchi's first migration, and he had no idea what to expect. It was exciting, but it was also sort of scary. He felt a pang as he looked over his shoulder at the nesting grounds, now vanishing in the distance. It was the place where he was born—the only place he'd ever known. Would he ever see it again?

My folk—the Alexornis birds—came along for the ride as well, naturally. Some of us flew alongside the Pachyrhinosaurus, perching in trees while we waited for our big friends to catch up. Others rode along on the Pachyrhinosaurus frills, clutching the bony ridges with our feet.

The Pachyrhinosaurus herds spread out to create an uneven line, with other, smaller dinosaurs falling into their company. The Parksosaurus darted nervously here and there. Everyone was on high alert. Fall often brought harsh, unpredictable weather, and there were thunderheads gathering. If the storm was bad, it would catch the whole herd out in the open, far from home.

THE CLIMATE AND GEOGRAPHY OF THE DINOSAURS

The Cretaceous Period—the final flourishing of the Age of Dinosaurs—was dramatically different from today. Cretaceous dinosaurs like *Tyrannosaurus*, *Gorgosaurus*, *Pachyrhinosaurus*, and *Troodon* lived in a hothouse world, in which temperatures were much higher than they are now. This extreme weather was probably a result of volcanoes. The Cretaceous was a time of intense volcanic eruptions, and the carbon dioxide belched out during these explosions would have heated the planet. Something similar is happening today, as our planet is rapidly warming because of the carbon dioxide produced by burning oil and coal.

Because temperatures were so high, there were probably no ice caps or glaciers over the polar regions during most of the Cretaceous Period. In turn, because little water was locked up in ice, more water was held in the oceans. Sea level was therefore much higher during the Cretaceous than it is today. During much of the Cretaceous Period, warm, shallow seas extended far onto the land, deep into the interiors of the continents. One such sea stretched all the way from the Gulf of Mexico to the Arctic Ocean, across the entire central part of North America!

As the herd moved farther south, a great storm began to build. Clouds streamed across the sky, casting dark shadows on Patchi and his family as they made their way through the vast plain. The wind picked up. As a distant rumble of thunder sounded, Bulldust turned decisively toward the woods, leading his family into the shelter and safety of the trees.

Patchi was trailing behind, as usual. Suddenly there was a terrific thunder clap, and lightning flashed—very nearby! Patchi jumped and scrambled to catch up with the others. The storm had arrived.

The Pachyrhinosaurus moved farther into the woods. The clouds were so thick now that it was as though the day had turned to night.

Soon the whole herd was in the woods, safe and sound—or that's what they thought. Me, I was worried. There was dry brush and dead trees everywhere. One lightning strike in the wrong place, and the whole forest would go up in flames.

Crash!

Well, I thought, there was the lightning strike. It had hit so near us that the sound of it and the flash of light came at exactly the same time. And immediately after the sound and the sight came the smell. A very bad, very scary smell.

Smoke.

Around me, the Pachyrhinosaurus flared their nostrils and rolled their eyes in fear. A forest fire during a lightning storm was bad news, and they knew it. Patchi made a scared little noise and moved closer to his mother.

The fire spread fast. Burning branches fell from the trees that had already caught fire, and soon the bed of pine needles and dry leaves on the ground was in flames, too. Smoke poured, thick and sour, through the forest.

The panicking animals fled. Everyone wanted to get out of the forest as fast as they could. The air was filled with

Alexornis birds flying away from the fire. Alphadon leaped from tree branch to tree branch to escape. On the ground, Ankylosaurus and Hesperonychus ran as fast as they could, crashing through the undergrowth. It was chaos.

Bulldust knew he had to lead the Pachyrhinosaurus away from the fire, too. He was responsible for the well-being of his entire herd, and that meant seeing them through this crisis to safety.

Bellowing loudly to gather his herd together, Bulldust led his family through the forest away from the fire. Smaller creatures darted in between the legs and sometimes even jumped across the backs of the lumbering Pachyrhinosaurus as they fled.

Patchi watched the creatures stampede through the forest, his eyes open wide. It was only when burning embers fell on the forest ground right in front of him, starting another fire, that he remembered to follow his herd. He ran to catch up with his mother.

The fire wasn't the only thing to worry about, either. In the chaos of the fire, hunters like the pterosaurs and Troodon were having a field day. The smaller creatures were too frightened of the fire to watch out for predators, and many of them were getting picked off as they fled through the forest.

PTEROSAURS

Pterosaurs—flying reptiles—are close cousins of dinosaurs. Many movies and books mistakenly call pterosaurs dinosaurs, but this is not true. They are not dinosaurs because they do not possess the defining features of dinosaurs, such as an open hip socket and large muscles on the upper arm bone. Instead, pterosaurs were one of many peculiar reptile groups that were very successful during the Mesozoic but are extinct today.

A typical pterosaur had a long skull with a sharp, pointed beak. The skull was probably topped by a thin crest, which was used to attract mates. The neck was long, and the forearms were modified into wings. The wings of pterosaurs differ from the wings of birds and bats. Most of the bird wing is made up of feathers, which attach to the bones of the arm. The wing of a bat is a thin, fleshy sheet of skin that extends between the fingers. Pterosaurs had a skin sheet similar to that of bats, except that it mostly extended backward from an elongated single finger, not between all of the fingers like in bats. This long finger of pterosaurs is equivalent to our ring finger. It is so enlarged that it is longer than the rest of the bones of the arm combined!

But the biggest, scariest predator in those woods was the Gorgosaurus. I watched as a Gorgosaurus quietly followed Patchi's herd through the woods. This was real trouble.

Crash! I forgot all about the Gorgosaurus as I watched a huge burning tree fall directly in the path of Bulldust's herd. The Pachyrhinosaurus scattered in all directions to avoid the enormous tree. When the dust settled, my heart sank.

On one side of the still-burning tree, Bulldust's herd made their way through the woods, fleeing the flames. On the other side, trapped by the blazing tree . . .

It was Patchi and Scowler! They'd been separated from their herd.

GORGOSAURUS

Gorgosaurus was a ferocious dinosaur that ate meat and walked on two legs, just like its famous cousin *Tyrannosaurus rex*. But *Gorgosaurus* was a bit smaller than *T. rex*. A full-grown adult was about twenty-six to twenty-nine feet long and weighed around two tons. It was also more slender than *T. rex*, with longer legs and the ability to run faster. If *T. rex* was an off-road jeep, *Gorgosaurus* was a Formula One car. Fossils of *Gorgosaurus* are commonly found in the Canadian province of Alberta and the American state of Montana. It would have lived about 77–74 million years ago, making it one of the first large tyrannosaurs to dominate the North American scene.

Gorgosaurus was a classic tyrannosaur. It had all of the familiar features of the group: a big skull, thick teeth, a long tail, and puny arms that were no bigger than the arms of a human! Scientists still debate what these arms could have been used for. *Gorgosaurus* was no weight lifter, that's for sure. But the arms must have been used for something, because although they were small, they were still quite strong and capable of a wide range of motion. Maybe they helped push the animal off the ground if it fell? Maybe they were used to grab onto a mate, or to build a nest? Or maybe to hold food close to the mouth? Ultimately we just don't know. Mysteries like this make paleontology an exciting science, like detective work in deep time.

wing. I had come to care about Patchi, and I couldn't bear to see him killed by one of those terrifying Gorgosaurus.

I braced myself for the worst.

Well, I thought Patchi and Scowler were goners for sure. But I'm telling you—Patchi was born under a lucky

star. The brothers dashed through a tangled pile of fallen trees, finally stopping to hide inside a hollow log. The pair had done enough to confuse the Gorgosaurus, which went in search of easier prey.

HOW DINOSAURS WENT EXTINCT

Scientists are sure that dinosaurs went extinct about 66 million years ago. Dinosaur fossils disappear at this time, all across the world. Rocks that were formed after 66 million years ago never contain dinosaur fossils. Something else also happened 66 million years ago. A huge asteroid about 6 miles wide smashed into present-day Mexico. There is a big crater, nearly 124 miles wide, that formed when the asteroid hit.

There were also some other weird things happening at the end of the Cretaceous Period, around the same time dinosaurs went extinct. Huge volcanic eruptions were occurring in present-day India. These were not the quick, explosive volcanic eruptions that we are used to in today's world. Instead, these eruptions produced a slow, steady flow of lava for thousands or maybe even millions of years. Today the remains of this lava cover over 190,000 square miles in India! This much lava would have produced a lot of toxic gas, which could have polluted the atmosphere and poisoned the dinosaurs.

Scientists continue to debate whether an asteroid or volcanoes was responsible for the death of the dinosaurs. Ultimately, we may never know for sure.

CHAPTER 5

In the morning, the two little dinosaurs awoke to silence. The sun was creeping slowly over the horizon as though it was afraid of what it would find.

It wasn't pretty. The forest was utterly transformed. Where there had been towering trees swaying in the wind, all there was now was a blackened plain of charred trunks and drifting white ash. It made my heart hurt to look at it.

Patchi and Scowler climbed out of their hiding place and looked around. The little Pachyrhinosaurus had no idea what to do. They were alone in the forest. Not another creature stirred in the utter desolation.

Patchi and Scowler were covered in mud and ash, but—amazingly—were unhurt. The brothers moved carefully over blackened logs, the charcoal crumbling under their feet. White ash spiraled and drifted in the wind. Soon they reached the edge of the forest. Patchi lifted his head, suddenly: He'd seen movement. A huge Pachyrhinosaurus walked past—then another. Patchi and Scowler began to run toward the other dinosaurs. Had they found their family?

When they got closer, they realized these were adults
from a different herd of Pachyrhinosaurus. The strangers
walked right by Patchi and Scowler, not even bothering
to look down at them. A herd would be unlikely to take
in two orphans from another herd, and these dinosaurs
clearly didn't plan on helping out my two little friends.

They were on their own.

I was never sure if Patchi or Scowler understood
their loss. Their father, mother, and siblings were gone.
Surviving without a family—without a herd—wouldn't
be easy.

Patchi and Scowler stood, shell-shocked, watching the
Pachyrhinosaurus herd pass them. One herd turned into
two, and soon there was an almost endless parade of
dinosaurs plodding through the broken, black charcoal
on their way south. Overhead, pterosaurs streamed by,
following the rest of the creatures to the Winter Ground.

DINOSAURS IN HERDS

Some dinosaurs were social creatures that gathered together in herds, packs, and other groups. Some dinosaurs may have herded together for protection or during migrations, while others may have formed packs for hunting. Scientists know that some dinosaurs formed social groups because of two very different types of fossil evidence.

First, paleontologists have discovered several dinosaur bone beds. These are huge fossil sites where the skeletons of many dinosaurs of the same species are jumbled together. Some of these bone beds contain more than a thousand skeletons! They also often include skeletons of juveniles, teenagers, and adults. The Late Cretaceous horned ceratopsids and duck-billed hadrosaurids are commonly found in bone beds. Even the large carnivorous tyrannosaurs *Albertosaurus* and *Tarbosaurus* have been found in smaller bone beds containing about ten skeletons. The fact that these dinosaurs are found in bone beds is strong evidence that they lived and died together. Ceratopsids and hadrosaurids probably formed huge herds that may have even migrated during the winter. Tyrannosaurs probably formed smaller hunting packs.

The second line of evidence comes from footprints. Sometimes tens of thousands of dinosaur footprints are found together at so-called megatracksites. These footprints mostly belong to the same species and are all facing in the same direction. This is strong evidence that these sites were formed by hundreds or thousands of members of a herd, traveling together and at about the same speed. The footprints of long-necked sauropods have been found in megatracksites, indicating that these dinosaurs herded together. Megatracksites are also known for some plant-eating ornithopod dinosaurs.

Many herds of Pachyrhinosaurus had passed Patchi and Scowler, when something caught Patchi's eye. A small, white shape flickered into sight and then disappeared. He looked again—there it was. A small female Pachyrhinosaurus was approaching. She was covered in white ash, like a ghost. She cocked her head, and the breeze lifted some of the ash off her skin.

Patchi couldn't believe it. It was Juniper—the young female Pachyrhinosaurus he'd met at the waterfall all those weeks ago! He hadn't expected to ever see her again, and now here she was.

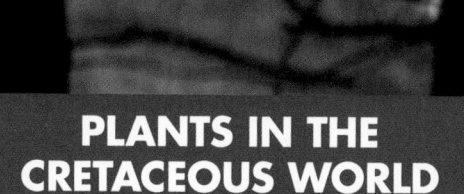

PLANTS IN THE CRETACEOUS WORLD

Something critical happened during the Cretaceous Period: The first flowering plants evolved. Flowering plants, technically known as angiosperms, are all of those plants with flowers and fruits. In today's world these include everything from grasses and oaks to palms, sunflowers, and cacti. Not all of these groups were around during the Cretaceous, but by the end of the period large trees such as magnolias were common, and the first grasses were spreading around the world. Meanwhile, other types of plants such as gymnosperms (the "evergreen" trees) and ferns were still diverse and provided a steady food source for plant-eating dinosaurs.

Patchi watched as Juniper marched along with the huge herd of assorted dinosaurs. She was following her mother.

It's a wonderful thing to find someone you know when you thought you were alone in the world. Patchi lost no time running after Juniper. Scowler followed his brother's lead, for once, and trotted along with him.

The threat from the fire was over, but the journey to survive had just begun. The dinosaurs still had a long way to travel before reaching the Winter Ground.

CHAPTER 6

Patchi and Scowler tagged along with the huge parade of dinosaurs heading south. They did their best to stay with Juniper. The weather began to worsen. Again. There were no more forest fires, but the rain was almost as miserable. It was a heavy, unending downpour. Curtains of rain swept through the valley and a cold wind buffeted the herd.

Patchi and Scowler did the best they could. With no adults to shelter or protect them, the two little dinosaurs had a hard time of it. The wind nearly knocked them over, and the cold rain froze them to the bone.

The downpour finally stopped, and the herd began their southward march once more. Patchi was distracted by

the beauty of the world after the rain—water sparkled on the ferns, and the sky was a deep, bright blue.

I took a deep breath and stretched my wings, letting the feathers dry in the sun. I was happy the weather had turned. I could tell the huge herd of dinosaurs was happy, too. The young ones played as the herd moved along, and the adults stepped more lightly.

Maybe, I thought, just maybe the rest of the journey will be easy.

How wrong I was.

No sooner had that thought crossed my mind, than I heard a faint sound from a hill nearby. I knew that sound, and it frightened me. It was the sound of a pack of Gorgosaurus. I watched in horror as they emerged from the trees at the top of the hill and hunkered down to spy on the herd below.

For a long time, the pack of Gorgosaurus waited, motionless. Below, the dinosaur herd continued grazing and wandering southward. They had no idea they were being watched—and they had no idea *who* was watching them.

MORE ABOUT *GORGOSAURUS*

Tyrannosaurs like *Gorgosaurus* were apex predators—they were at the top of the food chain and didn't have to worry about competition from smaller meat eaters. The skeleton of tyrannosaurs was well adapted for their carnivorous lifestyle. The huge skull boasted up to 70 thick, banana-sized teeth. Massive muscles powered the jaws. Some of the bones of the snout were fused together to give them extra strength. These features allowed tyrannosaurs to eat essentially whatever they wanted.

But tyrannosaurs could do more than just kill and eat their prey. They also did something truly bizarre: They crunched bone as they fed. Bite marks matching the size and shape of tyrannosaur teeth are known from several ceratopsid and hadrosaurid bones. These are not shallow scratches, but rather deep pits. So tyrannosaurs must have crunched right through the bones of their prey! This is confirmed by a study of tyrannosaur coprolites—fossilized dung—that are full of bone chunks. Bone crunching sets tyrannosaurs apart from most other animals, as this behavior is not known in other predatory dinosaurs or living reptiles. Some living mammals like hyenas, however, do regularly chomp through bone.

Gorgosaurus and *T. rex* are some of the largest and last surviving tyrannosaurs. Not all tyrannosaurs were so big, nor did they all live at the end of the Cretaceous Period. The tyrannosaur group evolved more than 100 million years before *T. rex*. The earliest tyrannosaurs like *Dilong*, *Guanlong*, and *Proceratosaurus* were human-sized animals that could run fast, but which lived in the shadow of other giant dinosaur predators like *Allosaurus* and *Spinosaurus*. Some of these early tyrannosaurs have even been found covered in feathers! This makes it most likely that *T. rex* and *Gorgosaurus* also would have had some sort of feathers on their body. Maybe they weren't fully feathered like a bird, but had a reduced coat of feathers much like an elephant has a thin coat of hair.

Finally, the biggest Gorgosaurus—the leader of the pack—gave the signal. Two male Gorgosaurus separated from the pack. They ran at full speed down the hillside, straight at the lumbering herd! I rose up into the air and sounded a warning: *Pee Hoo!* The herd spotted the Gorgosaurus and began to move, rushing away from the threat. All the dinosaurs in the herd clumped together for protection as they ran.

The two Gorgosaurus ran alongside the herd, waiting for an opening. And then the leader—the biggest Gorgosaurus—leapt out of hiding. He roared so loudly it echoed through the entire valley.

The careful, tightly packed retreat of the herd fell apart. They panicked, faced with this nightmare of a hunter. The herd stampeded, mindless and afraid. And the Gorgosaurus nipped at their heels. They were *herding* the other dinosaurs, I realized. They were directing the herd toward a raging river. The Gorgosaurus had a plan, and it wasn't a plan that would end well for Patchi's adopted herd.

With perfect timing and precision, the lead Gorgosaurus struck. He lunged at the stampeding herd, and separated out a small fraction of the group. These unlucky few were immediately pinned against the riverbank by the lead Gorgosaurus and his pack.

I almost couldn't bear to look, but I had to know. Was Patchi in that group?

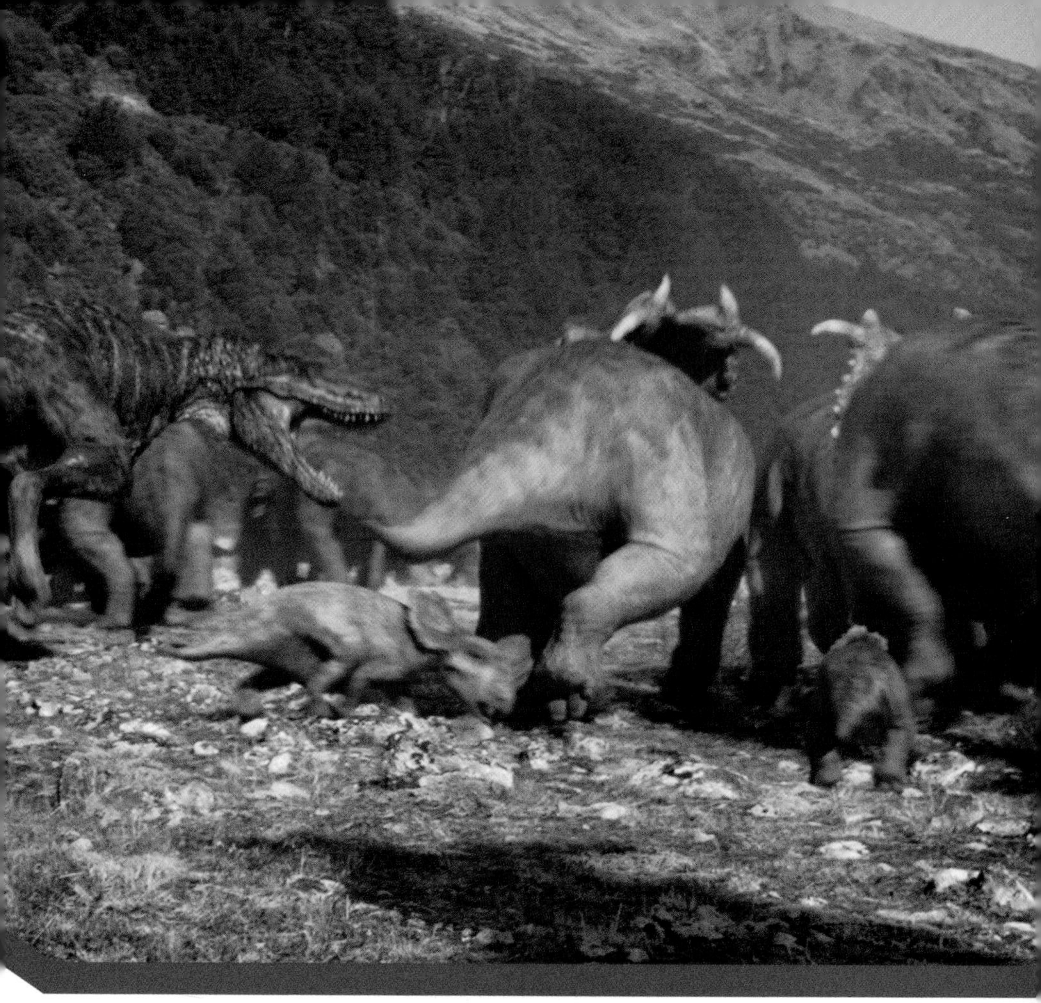

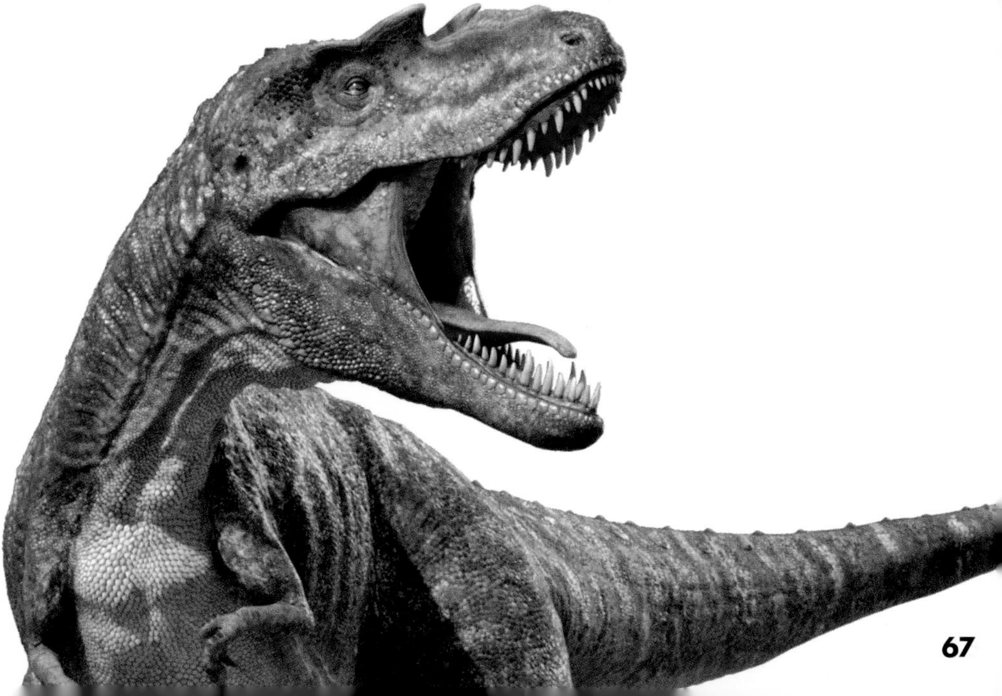

Yes. I spotted him and his brother Scowler . . . and Juniper, who had been separated from her mother. The three young ones crowded together. They hunkered down, terrified of the enormous, hungry hunters that threatened them.

MORE ABOUT *PACHYRHINOSAURUS*

Pachyrhinosaurus was an herbivore—an animal that ate only plants. Because it walked on four legs and didn't have a long neck, it would have fed on small bushes and shrubs growing on the ground. Ceratopsids like *Pachyrhinosaurus* were well adapted for eating plants. They had hundreds of small teeth in their jaws, which were packed tightly together so that each jaw had a long, sharp row of teeth. When the upper and lower jaws came together these rows would have sheared past each other like a pair of scissors. The packed tooth rows are called "dental batteries." They would have allowed ceratopsids to eat tough plants like evergreen leaves. They also would have allowed animals like *Pachyrhinosaurus* to quickly chop up a lot of plants before swallowing them. This was important, because ceratopsids were big animals and needed to eat a lot of food to stay active.

The adult Pachyrhinosaurus formed a line. They lowered their heads, and their bony frills created a barrier—like a wall of shields. There was a long, tense silence. Nobody moved. Then one adult Pachyrhinosaurus stepped forward, ready to do battle with the Gorgosaurus. It was an act of great courage.

I admired his bravery, but it was useless. The pack of Gorgosaurus was on him in a moment. The rest of the herd panicked, their defensive line forgotten. They ran in any direction they could, pushing and shoving one another in their fear.

Patchi was thrown to one side, then the other. He scrambled fast to keep from being trampled. And then suddenly, he, Scowler, and Juniper were on the edge of the river bank as it crumbled under the weight of so many dinosaurs.

The three young dinosaurs fell into the raging river and were carried downstream in a flash—far, far from their herd!

Patchi and Scowler were on their own again. And this time—so was Juniper.

CHAPTER 7

I watched helplessly as Patchi, Scowler, and Juniper were tossed from wave to wave. The little dinosaurs bobbed along in the water, sometimes disappearing under the surface. I could see the panic in their eyes— they were almost drowning!

Patchi's head popped up out of the water. He gasped for air, then disappeared again. The river frothed white with foam as it thundered along, taking him with it.

It was all the three Pachyrhinosaurus could do to stay alive as the river carried them out toward the sea.

By the time I caught up with them, they had washed up on a foggy beach. They were a sorry sight. Patchi was out cold, and Juniper's leg was badly injured. With no way to rejoin the herd, their chances of survival had gone from bad to worse. They had each other—but they were totally lost.

Patchi picked himself up and staggered over to check on Juniper. And that's when we all heard it—a distant cry, loud and long. It sounded like . . . could it be . . . ?

Edmontosaurus.

An entire herd of them—hundreds of these enormous creatures emerged out of the fog. They were making

their way south, too. These giants were intimidating, but they only ate plants—like the Pachyrhinosaurus did. Plus, they seemed to know where they were going.

EDMONTOSAURUS

Edmontosaurus was something like a dinosaur version of a horse. Large herds of these animals roamed across western North America at the end of the Cretaceous, chomping plants and dodging predators like *T. rex*. There isn't anything very fancy about the skeleton of *Edmontosaurus*. It didn't have any horns or spikes. Adults were large, but nothing like the size of the colossal long-necked sauropods. But what set *Edmontosaurus* apart was its speed (it could probably run at 20–25 miles per hour) and its incredible ability to eat a lot of plants very fast. Right at the end of the time of dinosaurs, when the asteroid smashed into Earth, *Edmontosaurus* was the most common and successful plant-eating dinosaur in all of North America.

During the very end of the Cretaceous Period, sauropod dinosaurs were rare in North America. It was duck-billed hadrosaurids like *Edmontosaurus* that were the largest plant eaters. These animals are distinguished from all other dinosaurs by their unusual skulls, which are very long, packed full of teeth, and fronted with a wide beak like that of a duck. *Edmontosaurus* is one of many hadrosaurid species that lived in North America and Asia in the Cretaceous, and it was among the biggest of these species. An average adult was about thirty feet long, but some individuals grew to about forty feet in length, the same size as *T. rex*! Most adults were about six to ten feet tall at the hips and weighed three to four tons. Just imagine the incredible amount of leaves and twigs such a big animal would need to eat. Herds of *Edmontosaurus* would probably chop down entire forests as they marched across the landscape!

The Edmontosaurus ignored Patchi, Scowler, and Juniper. They simply kept moving south, passing by the three little Pachyrhinosaurus without so much as looking at them.

I never thought of Patchi as a natural leader. He wasn't big or tough like his brother. But he knew there was strength in numbers. He knew how to keep moving

forward. So Patchi turned and started following the Edmontosaurus. Juniper was more hesitant. But she followed after him. Finally Scowler joined the two friends, and together they made their way, following the Edmontosaurus along the coast.

The three little dinosaurs stayed with the
Edmontosaurus for a long way down the beach. Scowler,
always headstrong and tireless, had no trouble keeping
up. But Juniper's leg was badly hurt. She limped along
as fast as she could, but soon she was falling behind.
Patchi looked ahead at his strong, confident brother, safe
with the Edmontosaurus herd. Then he looked back at
Juniper, afraid and in pain. His decision was made.

He hung back with Juniper. Together, the two
friends moved slowly—much slower than their traveling
companions. Gradually, they fell to the back of the
herd. It wasn't too long before they watched the herd of
Edmontosaurus vanish in the distance.

They were alone again.

Unable to move any farther, Juniper collapsed on the sand. Patchi nosed at her, worried. But he sprang back when a bright red crab emerged from underneath a nearby log. Soon, the two friends were surrounded by

crabs! The crustaceans danced back and forth, waving their pincers. Patchi was entranced—the world was full of new things to learn about.

But the show ended suddenly—too suddenly—when a pterosaur appeared. The huge winged reptile dived out of the sky and landed on the ground right in front of Patchi and Juniper!

The pterosaur struck fast, its long, pointed beak snapping up one of the crabs. Then another pterosaur appeared, and the two winged giants began hunting crabs in earnest. Patchi and Juniper snuck quietly away, happy to be ignored. The pterosaurs could just as easily have made a meal of *them*.

WHAT ELSE LIVED WITH DINOSAURS?

Living alongside the dinosaurs on land was a range of crocodiles, lizards, snakes, mammals, and pterosaurs. Pterosaurs—the familiar flying reptiles of the Mesozoic—evolved in the Triassic and lasted until the end of the Cretaceous Period. They are close relatives of dinosaurs, but not true dinosaurs. The oldest mammals also evolved in the Triassic. Mammals remained mostly small throughout the Mesozoic Era, rarely reaching sizes larger than a fox. They were overshadowed by the dinosaurs for over 100 million years, but finally had their chance to dominate after the dinosaurs went extinct. Mesozoic crocodiles were nothing like today's crocodiles. Whereas all living species are pretty much the same—they are slow-moving sprawlers that lurk near the edge of the water to ambush prey—Mesozoic crocodiles included fast runners, plant eaters, and even fully ocean-living species.

The Mesozoic oceans were teeming with life. Whales had yet to evolve, and sharks had not reached the great sizes seen today. The top predators in Mesozoic oceans and seas were mostly reptiles. The long-necked plesiosaurs prospered during much of the Jurassic and Cretaceous Periods. They used their paddles to fly through the water, and some species reached huge sizes, maybe even larger than *Tyrannosaurus rex*. During the latest Cretaceous, when warm seas covered most of the continents and plesiosaurs were in decline, another group of fierce predatory reptiles evolved: the mosasaurs. Meanwhile, throughout much of the Mesozoic, the dolphin-like ichthyosaurs lived across the globe. These fast-swimming reptiles probably ate mostly shellfish and other smaller creatures, but some might have been top predators as well.

Patchi and Juniper made their way off the beach and into the woods as fast as they could. The journey would be slower in the woods, but the trees would shelter them from predators like pterosaurs.

Patchi led the way, some deep instinct pointing him south. Behind him, Juniper limped along. Her bad leg slowed her down even more in the dark. The forest floor was uneven and slippery. She fell and got up again, and fell again.

All around them, the night air was full of strange noises. The forest seemed to close in on the two Pachyrhinosaurus. They were too young to be alone, too small . . . and they were afraid. But they kept moving.

Patchi stepped over a tree root, and froze in shock when it moved. Juniper's eyes widened. In the dim moonlight of the forest, they could see now that it wasn't a tree root at all. It was a Gorgosaurus tail! Patchi was standing between the tail and hind legs of a sleeping Gorgosaurus. Its mouth was open as it snored, and its razor-sharp teeth gleamed in the moonlight.

Very carefully, very quietly, Patchi moved away from the sleeping monster. Once he was clear, he ran, Juniper following him. They didn't slow down until they were well away from the Gorgosaurus.

But the Gorgosaurus wasn't the only creature in the woods that evening. As Patchi and Juniper hurried through the forest, a pair of glowing orange eyes watched them go. Then another pair, and another. Soon, the two friends were surrounded. Juniper and Patchi skidded to a halt. There were Chirostenotes all around them. These creatures weren't normally dangerous, but they were a lot bigger than Patchi and Juniper. And they were mad. They hovered around the two young dinosaurs, clucking and hissing.

Patchi had had enough. After days of being frightened and attacked, he decided to fight back! He lunged at one Chirostenotes, biting at its leg. He pushed another one with his bony head. Inspired by his bravery, Juniper fought back, too. Soon, the two baby Pachyrhinosaurus had the Chirostenotes on the run!

CHIROSTENOTES

Oviraptorosaurs are some of the most bizarre dinosaurs ever to have lived. They look more like aliens out of a bad science fiction movie than an actual living, breathing type of animal. They were theropods—members of that great group of carnivorous dinosaurs that includes *Tyrannosaurus* and *Velociraptor*—but they probably didn't eat meat all of the time. Most species had no teeth, but their jaws were covered with a sharp beak like that of a bird.

Chirostenotes is one of the best known oviraptorosaurs. It lived in North America during the final 10–12 million years of the Cretaceous Period, alongside *Tyrannosaurus*, *Triceratops*, and many other iconic dinosaurs. It was one of the smaller dinosaurs in its ecosystem. Most individuals were about five to seven feet long from head to tail and three to six and a half feet tall at the hips. While it is difficult to estimate exactly, they probably didn't weigh much. Many bones of their skeleton were hollowed out and filled with air sacs, which would have reduced the weight of the animal. This is just one of many birdlike features of *Chirostenotes* and other oviraptorosaurs. In fact, these dinosaurs are some of the closest relatives to birds. They are more closely related to birds than dinosaurs like *Brachiosaurus*, *Triceratops*, and *Tyrannosaurus*, but not quite as closely related as small, fast-running theropods like *Troodon* and *Velociraptor*.

Fossils tell us that *Chirostenotes* had long legs well suited for running, and huge arms that ended in large, pointed claws. The claws may have been used to capture prey, or perhaps for defense. There is still much debate about what *Chirostenotes* and its relatives ate. They certainly didn't eat meat in the same style that *Tyrannosaurus* and *Velociraptor* did, because they didn't have any teeth to cut or slice their prey. They may have eaten smaller mammals and lizards, or perhaps their strong skulls and beaks were adapted for eating hard foods like nuts or eggs.

Patchi and Juniper ran up the wooded slope, away from the Gorgosaurus. Away from the Chirostenotes. Toward a beautiful glow in the sky.

As they reached the top of the hill, the trees thinned and the two friends saw something amazing: The Arctic night sky was lit up by the aurora borealis. The

Northern Lights shimmered and faded across the sky, casting a greenish light over the valley below them.

CHAPTER 8

Patchi and Juniper stared up at the sky. They had never seen the Northern Lights before. Then they looked down and they were even more amazed.

The valley below them was filled with the mixed herds from the North Slopes. All the creatures that had left the Arctic Circle to find a home for the winter were there. Against all odds, Patchi and Juniper had found the Winter Ground! Their journey was over.

THE WORLD OF THE DINOSAURS

The Earth is always changing. The animals and plants that are alive today have not always been around. The climate we are used to is different from the climate the dinosaurs would have experienced. Mountains rise up and are then eroded to dust, volcanoes erupt and then go dry, and rivers change course. The story of the Earth is a 4.54-billion-year story of change.

Not even the land we live on is stable. The seven continents of today's world have not always been in the same position. They have moved around over time. The understanding that continents move was one of the great discoveries of twentieth-century science. This idea is called continental drift. Continents move because the surface of the Earth is divided into several segments called plates. These plates slide against one another, creating earthquakes. They also move apart from each other in some places, forming oceans between them, and collide together in other places, creating mountains. Movement of the plates is driven by intense heat in the interior of the Earth. Sometimes this heat escapes to the surface through volcanoes.

Dinosaurs lived on continents that were very different from our own. The first dinosaurs lived on the supercontinent Pangaea: a single landmass created when many smaller continents merged together. Pangaea began to break apart about 200 million years ago, as the Atlantic Ocean formed between North America and Europe. The intense volcanic eruptions that accompanied this violent split caused the great extinction at the end of the Triassic period. During the next 100 million years the continents continued to split and move. South America, Africa, Australia, Antarctica, and India remained sutured together for much of the Age of Dinosaurs, but began to break apart from each other during the Cretaceous Period. North America and Asia also split during this time. By the end of the Age of Dinosaurs, some 66 million years ago, the continents basically were located in the same places they are today.

Patchi and Juniper didn't waste any time. They hurried down the slope, skidding on the snow. As they got closer, they saw a familiar face. There, grazing with the Edmontosaurus, was Scowler! He'd made it to the Winter Ground. But Patchi and Juniper made a beeline for the Pachyrhinosaurus.

Even a birdbrain like me knows when he's looking at a happy ending. All three of the young Pachyrhinosaurus had made it to the Winter Ground alive—against all the odds. I was proud of those kids. Especially Patchi. I couldn't have been prouder if I'd hatched him from an egg myself.

It seems absurd, I know. But in fact, there's a very strong connection between birds and dinosaurs—and there always has been. Just as the Pachyrhinosaurus continued their line in babies like Patchi and Juniper, so the dinosaurs live on in birds—birds just like me.

DINOSAURS AND BIRDS

The idea that birds evolved from dinosaurs is probably the single most important fact ever discovered by dinosaur paleontologists. It is not a new idea, although it has been strongly supported by a wealth of new fossil discoveries over the past twenty years.

Scientists first noted the amazing similarity between dinosaurs and birds in the 1860s, when a fossil of the oldest known bird was discovered in Germany. This 150-million-year-old bird, which was called *Archaeopteryx*, was covered in a coat of feathers and had a wishbone, both characteristic features of birds that are not known in any other living animal. But it also had teeth and a long tail, neither of which is seen in any living bird. *Archaeopteryx*, therefore, seems to have been a mixture of dinosaur and bird!

Over the next 130 years scientists discovered several other important fossils that supported the link between dinosaurs and birds. But the most remarkable discoveries did not come to light until the 1990s. Deep in the farmlands of northeastern China, villagers began to find strange fossil bones surrounded by feather impressions. These were true dinosaurs—animals very closely related to *Velociraptor* and *Tyrannosaurus*. But they were covered in feathers. And there weren't just one or two fossils, but tens of thousands. Today, the "feathered dinosaurs" of China are the most beautiful and visual proof that birds evolved from dinosaurs. This idea is no longer seriously debated among scientists. It has become scientific fact.

Scientists accept this theory because there is a huge amount of evidence to support it. Feathered dinosaurs are the most obvious, but there are also other clues. Living birds share hundreds of features of the skeleton with dinosaurs, including things like wishbones, a wrist that can fold against the body (to protect the wing), and hollow bones, which are filled with extensions of the lung called air sacs. None of these things are seen in any animals other than birds and dinosaurs. There is behavioral evidence as well. Amazing dinosaur fossils have been found on top of nests, protecting their eggs in the same style as living birds. Microscopic studies of dinosaur bones show that dinosaurs grew fast like living birds. And the evidence goes on and on. So when you look out at a flock of geese, or a pigeon strutting around town, you are actually looking at a dinosaur!